Care for Our World

written by Karen Robbins   illustrated by Alexandra Ball

COMPENDIUM
kids

inspiring possibilities.

With special thanks to the entire Compendium family.

Written by: Karen Robbins
Illustrated by: Alexandra Ball
Designed by: Steve Potter
Edited by: M.H. Clark & Dan Zadra
Creative Direction by: Sarah Forster

Library of Congress Control Number: 2011942686
ISBN: 978-1-935414-61-2

1st printing. Printed in China with soy inks.

To my Mom and Dad, who taught me to care.

–Karen Robbins

Dedicated to Tom Scrivner, a true monkey at heart
and the bravest man I'll ever know.

–Alexandra Ball

Care for our world,
for you and for me,
for all living things
from mountain to sea.

For blossoms and berries and veggies that grow, for orchards and forests, and grass that we mow.

For kittens and ponies,
rabbits and puppies.

For turtles and hamsters, goldfish and guppies.

Care for all creatures no matter how small;
the Earth's their backyard and home for us all.

For spiders and butterflies,
cute lady bugs,
for scampering crickets
and slippery slugs.

For raccoons and beavers
and curly horned sheep,
for black bears with cubs
in deep winter sleep.

For schools of bright fish and crawling crabs too,
for sharks and for flounders
in oceans so blue.

This Earth is the one place
that all of us share,
so let's work together
and show how we care.

For jaguars and toucans,
for frogs, snakes, and bees,

for sloths with three toes who hang from the trees.

For tigers and camels,
big elephants too.
For black-and-white pandas,
munching bamboo.

For lions and leopards and graceful giraffes,

hyenas and monkeys who make us all laugh.

Our world is so big
that by now you must know:
You have friends to discover
wherever you go.

Care for kangaroos, emus, and bush wallabies,
for big furry wombats, koalas in trees.

For brave daddy penguins,
with eggs on their feet.
For seals and blue whales
who dive down to eat.

Please care for all people,
and all living things
with leaves, legs, or feathers,
arms, fins, or wings.

This is their world,
and it's yours and it's mine.
If we all treat it gently,
it will last a long time.

This world is our home. We need one another.

Please care for our world; we're sisters and brothers.